DETECTIVE PAW OF THE LAW

The Case of the Missing Painting

Time to Read™ is an early reader program designed to guide children to literacy success regardless of age or grade level. The program's three levels correspond to stages of reading readiness, making book selection straightforward, and assuring that when it's time for a child to read, the right book is waiting.

Level 1 — **Beginning to Read**
- Large, simple type
- Basic vocabulary
- Word repetition
- Strong illustration support

Level 2 — **Reading with Help**
- Short sentences
- Engaging stories
- Simple dialogue
- Illustration support

Level 3 — **Reading Independently**
- Longer sentences
- Harder words
- Short paragraphs
- Increased story complexity

Also by Dosh Archer

DETECTIVE PAW OF THE LAW

The Case of the Missing Painting

Dosh Archer

Albert Whitman & Company
Chicago, Illinois

To Jacquie and Chris with love

Library of Congress Cataloging-in-Publication data
is on file with the publisher.

Text and illustrations copyright © 2019 by Dosh Archer
First published in the United States of America
in 2019 by Albert Whitman & Company
ISBN 978-0-8075-1559-4

Printed in China
10 9 8 7 6 5 4 3 2 1 WKT 22 21 20 19 18

Design by Ellen Kokontis

For more information about Albert Whitman & Company,
visit our website at www.albertwhitman.com.

Prologue

In the heart of Big City is Big City
Police Headquarters, home to the Big
City Police Force.

This is where Detective Paw works
with his assistant, Patrol Officer Prickles.

Detective Paw never gives up when
investigating a crime. He has been
a detective for a very long time. His

mother and father were detectives
before him. He can outsmart any
criminal with his brilliant brain.

Patrol Officer Prickles is brave and
loyal and has all the latest police-issue

crime-fighting equipment. He is always there to help Detective Paw.

Together they solve crime; that's what they love doing…although it's not always easy.

Chapter One

It had been raining all night and was still cloudy when Detective Paw arrived at his office on Saturday morning. As he sat down, his phone rang.

It was Patrol Officer Prickles.

"It's Patrol Officer Prickles here. A painting is missing from an exhibition at New West End Gallery. Can you get here as soon as possible to help solve the crime?"

"Secure the scene, Prickles," said Detective Paw. "I'm on my way."

Detective Paw grabbed his notebook and pencil (for writing down clues) and magnifying glass (for  spotting teeny-tiny clues), and jumped in his Vintagemobile. He put the blue flashy light on the top and sped to the scene of the crime.

"The scene is secure, sir," said Patrol Officer Prickles, who was waiting for him inside the gallery.

"Excellent work," said Detective Paw. "Fill me in on what's happened."

Patrol Officer Prickles took out his latest police-issue electronic notepad. "I arrived at the scene of the crime at 8:31 a.m. I was responding to a call from Felicity Flusterfeathers, the owner of the gallery and organizer of the exhibition. She called to say there was a painting missing. I noticed the following things:

 **1.** There was a small puddle of water on the floor.

2. The skylight was open.

 **3.** There is a handle inside on the wall that opens the skylight.

4. There were some muddy tire tracks outside at the back of the gallery."

"Well done, Prickles," said Detective Paw. "Good work."

He turned to Felicity Flusterfeathers.

"Good morning, Miss Flusterfeathers. Tell me more about the situation."

"The exhibition is called *Spots and Stripes*," said Felicity. "Featuring two artists: Yurika Catimoto and Leonardo Smith. The three of us spent last evening hanging the paintings. This morning, when I unlocked the doors, I saw a painting was missing. Later today we are having a press conference and a grand opening here at the gallery. The press conference was supposed

to be for the artists to talk about
their work, but somehow the press
has already heard about the missing
painting. It is all they are interested in.
This will be on the front page of every
newspaper!"

Everyone looked at the space on the wall where the painting had been.

"I am so upset," cried Felicity Flusterfeathers.

"Calm down," said Detective Paw, popping a peppermint into his mouth to help him think. "I will get to the bottom of this."

Chapter Two

"I must ask you, Miss Flusterfeathers," said Detective Paw. "Where were you last night after you and the artists hung the paintings?"

"I walked home before it started raining, and then I went to bed early," said Felicity. "Organizing this exhibition has been tiring. I'm no spring chicken."

"Thank you, Miss Flusterfeathers. Please go and wait in the office. I must talk with Patrol Officer Prickles."

"It seems to me," said Detective Paw to Patrol Officer Prickles, "the gallery is getting a lot of press attention because of this. I must investigate further."

Detective
Paw went
outside to
look at the tire
tracks. They were
very big.

"Hmm," said Detective Paw, "that sure is interesting for my investigation." He made some notes. "See how deep the tire tracks are? This must have been a big vehicle."

Patrol Officer Prickles took a photograph of the tracks with his latest police-issue camera.

Back in the gallery, Detective Paw inspected the puddle and the handle

on the wall. He twiddled his mustache thoughtfully.

"That skylight can only be opened and closed from the inside," he said. "It is possible that someone got in and out through the skylight, but they couldn't close it properly. That meant during the night the rain got in and caused the puddle."

"But the skylight is so high up," said Patrol Officer Prickles.

"It sure is," said Detective Paw. "For someone to get up there they would need a ladder, or possibly a climbing rope."

YURIKA
CATIMOTO

Chapter Three

Detective Paw spoke to Felicity again.

"Tell me more about the artists," said Detective Paw.

"Yurika Catimoto paints spots. She is famous. Have you heard of her?"

"Of course," said Patrol Officer Prickles. "She is my favorite artist."

"Leonardo Smith is an up-and-coming

painter," said Felicity Flusterfeathers. "He paints stripes. I try to give new artists like him a chance. It is his painting that is missing. It is called *The Horizontal and the Vertical.*" She showed Detective Paw a photograph of the painting on her phone.

"What is that squiggle in the corner?" asked Detective Paw.

"That is Leonardo's signature," said Felicity. "Artists sign their work so we know it's really theirs."

"Please send a photograph of the painting to Patrol Officer Prickles," said Detective Paw. "For investigative purposes."

Patrol Officer Prickles stood by to receive the data on his latest police-issue phone.

"I will also need the addresses of the artists," said Detective Paw. "I need to interview them."

They set off for Yurika Catimoto's studio first. Outside, there was a spotty bicycle.

Yurika answered the door.

"May I help you, gentlemen?" she asked.

"One of Leonardo's paintings has been stolen, and I need to ask you some

questions," said Detective Paw. "Can you tell us where you were last night?"

"Here, painting through the night," said Yurika. "A great artist never sleeps. My assistant, Mr. Matsumoto, will confirm this. He was helping."

"Yes," said Mr. Matsumoto, trying to hide a yawn. "I washed all the brushes over and over."

"I take it you will be at the press conference this afternoon?" asked Detective Paw.

"Of course," said Yurika. "You don't think I stole Leonardo's painting, do you? I was trying to help him by allowing him to exhibit with me."

"With all due respect, ma'am," said Detective Paw. "I have not finished my investigation. Oh, and by the way, is that your bicycle outside?"

"Why yes," said Yurika. "I am just about to cycle to the press conference now."

"Thank you, ma'am," said Detective Paw. "I will be in touch."

They left for Leonardo's studio.

Leonardo answered the door. He was on his cell phone.

"Yes," he cried into the phone. "I am devastated. It was my masterpiece! I cannot talk anymore. The police have arrived."

"Who were
you just talking
to?" asked
Detective Paw.
*Big City
Daily News*,"
said Leonardo.
"Hmm,"
said Detective
Paw, "you sure
are getting a lot of attention over this.
Where were you last night?"

"After hanging the paintings, I came
home," said Leonardo. "Then I did some
yoga and went to bed."

Leonardo's phone rang again. As

Detective Paw and Patrol Officer Prickles were leaving they heard him say, "Is that the *Daily Trumpet*? Yes, I *am* devastated!"

Outside, Detective Paw turned to Patrol Officer Prickles. "I have three suspects. All with a reason to take

the painting. One of them has told the press about what happened. Who could it be? Each of them would benefit from the press attention. It would help the exhibition become very well known. And as for Leonardo, he is getting the most attention. He has become famous!"

Detective Paw twiddled his mustache. "This is a two-peppermint problem." He popped another peppermint into his mouth to help him think extra hard.

After he had thought extra hard, he said, "I do not think Miss Flusterfeathers did it. She would not want people to think her gallery was unsafe. Otherwise other artists might not want to show

their paintings in it. As for Yurika
Catimoto, it could not be her because
she has a spotty bicycle, not a big
vehicle. Also she was working with Mr.
Matsumoto all night. Let's go back to the
art gallery and talk to them all together."

Chapter Four

Back at the gallery, the press conference was just starting. Outside, Detective Paw saw Yurika's bicycle, and then he noticed an SUV parked nearby.

He walked around the SUV. "Look," he said. "The tires are muddy, and in the back there is a climbing rope. Prickles, compare these tire tracks with the photographs of the tracks you took before."

Patrol Officer Prickles did so. "Sir, they are the same," he said.

"Find out who owns this vehicle, Prickles," said Detective Paw.

Patrol Officer Prickles used his latest police-issue mobile license scanner to read the license plate. Then he sent the

details to police headquarters. Within minutes, he received the name of the owner of the SUV.

"It is just as I suspected," said Detective Paw when Prickles showed him the information.

When Detective Paw and Prickles came through the doors of the gallery, Leonardo was showing off a new painting.

"This is my next masterpiece," he said. "It will never replace the one that was stolen, but I hope you all like it. It is called *The Vertical and the Horizontal*."

"Stop right there!" cried Detective Paw. "You are under arrest!"

"What for?" said Leonardo.

"Taking your own painting," said Detective Paw.

Everyone turned
to look at Detective
Paw. The cameras
started flashing.

"The evidence
is clear," said
Detective Paw. He turned to the press.

"Someone came and
took the painting in the
night. The skylight was
open, and it was opened
from the inside, so it was
someone who was in the gallery the
night before. There were
muddy tire tracks at the
back of the gallery this

morning that match the muddy tires on the SUV outside. And that SUV belongs to—Leonardo Smith! That proves he was out at night after it had rained enough to make the ground muddy. There is a climbing rope in his SUV. He must have used it to climb in."

"If I stole it, where's the painting?" cried Leonardo.

Detective Paw pointed at the "new" painting. In the corner was Leonardo's signature. It was upside down.

"Prickles, turn the painting the right way up," said Detective Paw. Prickles did so.

"And now we can see that this painting is, in fact, *The Horizontal and the Vertical*. Leonardo has tried to pass off the painting he took for a new one by turning it upside down!"

Leonardo knew the game was up.

"The exhibition should have been called *Stripes and Spots*," he cried. "I should have come first. I am a genius, yet Yurika gets all the glory. I had to make sure I got noticed, so I was very daring. I opened the skylight while we were hanging the paintings and drove to the gallery in the middle of the night, climbed up on the rope, in through the skylight, and took my painting. Now everyone knows about me! I would have gotten away with it if it hadn't been for these two troublesome cops."

Patrol Officer Prickles put Leonardo in the back of his car and drove him to the station where Detective Paw had stern words for him.

"You wanted fame, Leonardo, but it is better to become well known because you have worked hard and done good things, not by tricking and telling

lies. You will have to see Judge Joan. She will decide what your punishment is. I will tell her you pretended to steal your own painting, went into the gallery without

permission, and wasted police time."

Leonardo left the station feeling very sorry and very worried about seeing Judge Joan.

"Brilliant detective work," said Patrol Officer Prickles to Detective Paw.

"I couldn't have done it without you, Prickles," said Detective Paw.

Thanks to Detective Paw's clue-spotting genius and the skilled use of gadgets by Patrol Officer Prickles, the case was solved. The sun had come out. It was going to be a sunny Saturday after all.